MW00903082

THANK YOU
FOR CHOOSING THIS BOOK
BEING PART OF YOUR LIFE

DISCLAIMER / COPYRIGHT

ALL RIGHTS RESERVED@. NO PART OF THIS BOOK MAY BE REPRODUCED, STORED
IN RETRIEVEL SYSTEM OR TRANSMITTED IN ANY FORM
OR BY ANY MEANS, ELECTRONIC, MECHANICAL,
PHOTOCOPYING, RECORDING OR OTHERWISE WITHOUT THE PRIOR
WRITTEN PERMISSION OF THE AUTHOR.

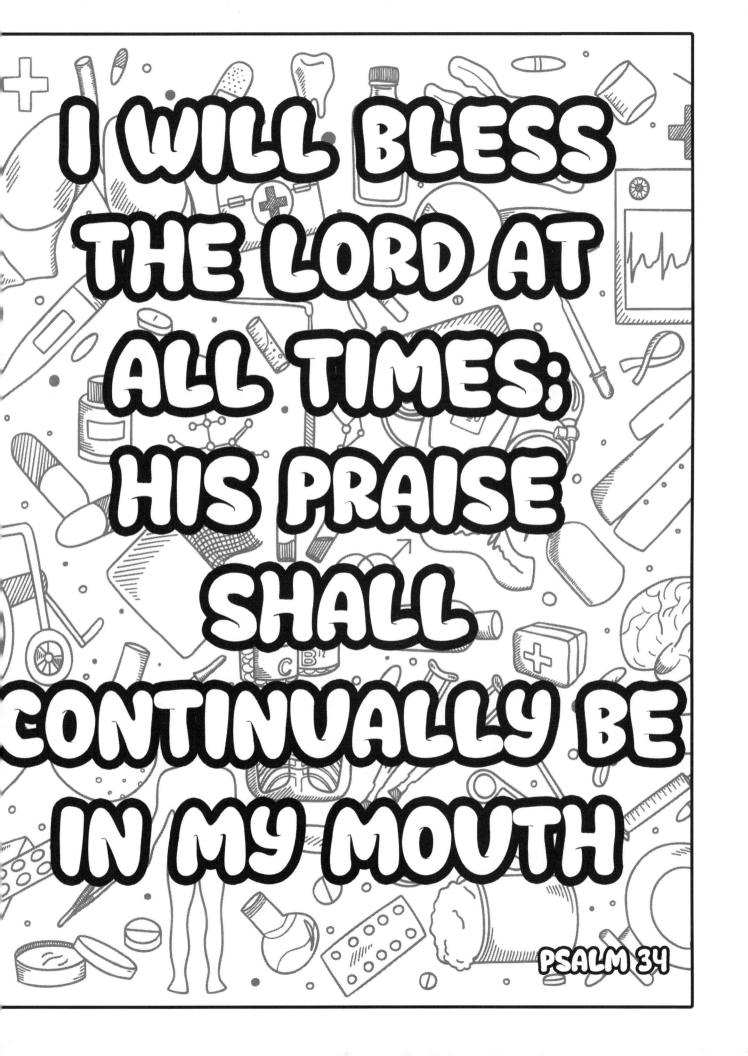

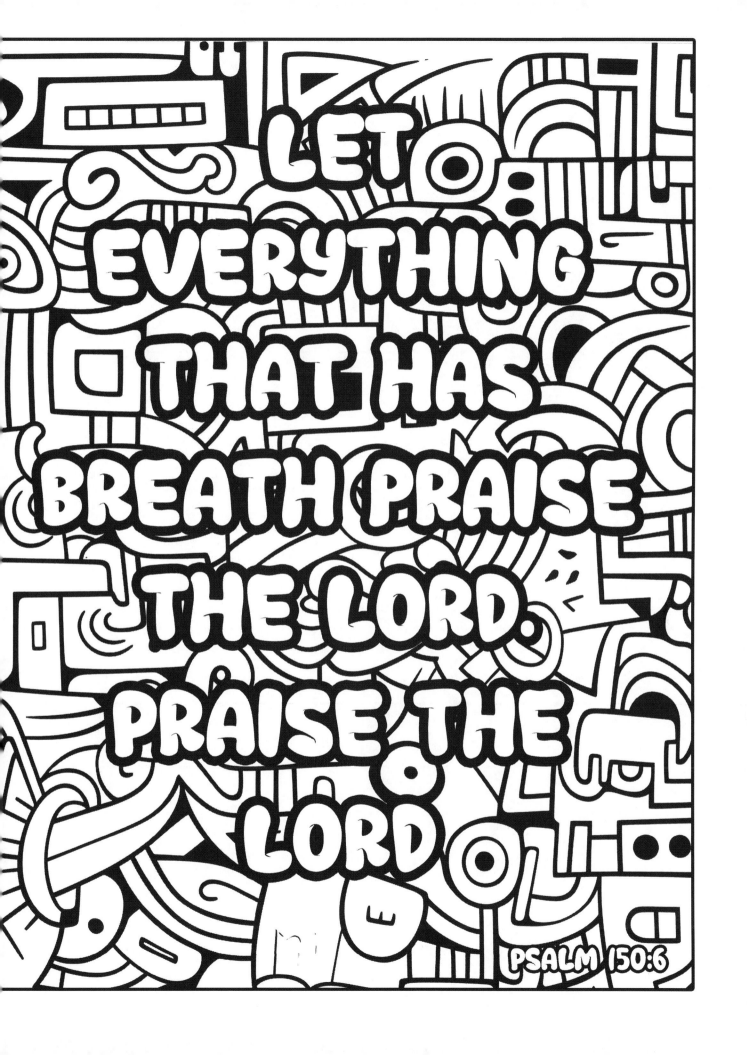

THROUGH THE PRAISE OF CHILDREN AND INFANTS YOU HAVE ESTABLISHED A STRONGHOLD AGAINST YOUR ENEMIES, TO SILENCE THE FOE AND THE AVENGER.

PSALM 8:2

YOUR WORD IS A LAMP TO MY FEET AND A LIGHT TO MY PATH

PSALM 119:105

@ **2023** SMMBYV

Author Name : Sebastian Vogel
Address   : 90610 Winkelhaid, Germany
FB   : https://www.facebook.com/SMMBYV/
Mail   : smmbyv@gmail.com

Made in United States
Orlando, FL
05 July 2024

48647388R00046

MW00903083

Happy the Lion

Karin Ahrenholz

Illustrated by Heather Keys

Copyright © 2019 Karin Ahrenholz.

All rights reserved. No part of this book may be used or reproduced by any means, graphic, electronic, or mechanical, including photocopying, recording, taping or by any information storage retrieval system without the written permission of the author except in the case of brief quotations embodied in critical articles and reviews.

Interior Image Credit: Heather Keys

Balboa Press books may be ordered through booksellers or by contacting:

Balboa Press
A Division of Hay House
1663 Liberty Drive
Bloomington, IN 47403
www.balboapress.com
1 (877) 407-4847

Because of the dynamic nature of the Internet, any web addresses or links contained in this book may have changed since publication and may no longer be valid. The views expressed in this work are solely those of the author and do not necessarily reflect the views of the publisher, and the publisher hereby disclaims any responsibility for them.

Any people depicted in stock imagery provided by Getty Images are models, and such images are being used for illustrative purposes only.
Certain stock imagery © Getty Images.

ISBN: 978-1-9822-2586-5 (sc)
ISBN: 978-1-9822-2587-2 (e)

Library of Congress Control Number: 2019904287

Print information available on the last page.

Balboa Press rev. date: 04/15/2019

BALBOA
PRESS
A DIVISION OF HAY HOUSE

Happy
the Lion

Once upon a time there was a lion named Happy. He was born with a smile on his face.

He was the happiest lion in the pride. Whenever he was around the other lions, they were all happy too. He could even get the grumpy old lions to crack a smile.

As Happy grew older, he learned the ways of the pride. Each time he learned something new he wondered why they did it that way. When he tried to change things and do them his way, he would get scolded. They would say to him, this is the way lions have always done it Happy, and since you are a lion, you should do it too. They also said that if he wasn't going to do things the way the pride did them, then he would have to leave.

Happy's mother could tell that something was wrong. She said, "You must always pay attention to the way you feel." If you are not happy, you need to think about what you can do to be happy. No one else can do it for you.

After lying awake for several hours thinking about how he was feeling, Happy finally fell into a deep sleep. He dreamed about a beautiful white bird. In his dream she taught him how to be happy again.

The next morning, he woke up and said to himself, I am going to do what feels right to me. I need to leave the pride to find a way to be happy again. And then he thought, maybe I will find that white bird from my dream....

So, Happy headed out into the forest, alone. He walked for a very long time on a bumpy path. He stubbed his toe on a rock. It started raining and continued for many days. He had no idea where he could find happiness.

Suddenly, Happy lost his footing and began sliding, out of control, down a muddy hillside. He flew into the air and landed into the middle of a raging river! After being carried by the rushing water for a while, Happy managed to swim over to the bank and crawl out.

He fell to the grass and said, "I give up." He slept for a long time. When he woke up, he had more energy and felt a little better, so he decided to keep going. He thought, things can only get better from here.

As the sun was setting, he came up to a very large tree where something shiny caught his eye. He looked closer and suddenly jumped back. What was that?!? He looked again and saw a scraggly lion who looked very sad. He stood there for a while and realized that it was his own reflection, in a mirror, and he looked just the way he felt.

He was startled when something moved next to him. He looked over and saw the most beautiful bird he had ever seen. It was the bird from his dream! His heart skipped a beat. She said, "Hello, my name is Tori, what's yours?" "Happy," grunted the lion. Tori laughed and said, "Well, you don't look Happy."

It was late, and he was too tired to explain, so Happy sulked away and fell asleep.

The next morning Tori was next to Happy when he awoke and he was glad to see her there. They talked all day about so many things. Tori was very wise and beautiful. She told Happy that she looked the way she felt. Happy told her that he left the pride to find a way to be happy again. Tori said he didn't need to leave the pride to find it, but now that he was here, she would show him how.

Happy told Tori that he dreamed he met her and that she taught him how to be happy again. "And here I am" said Tori."In order for you to be happy you need to start thinking about things that make you happy when you think about them. Can you think of anything?" It was hard for him to do since he was so sad.

Tori said to try and think of things that are easy to be happy about, like the fresh air to breathe and this beautiful day. She continued filling his head with lovely thoughts until he started to smile. Happy thoughts were all in his head and suddenly, he was feeling much happier.

They continued this friendship for several months being happy and having fun together. Then one day, Happy glanced over at the mirror and walked closer to see the gorgeous, majestic, lion he had become. He knew in that moment that he looked exactly the way he felt. His heart was full and he took a deep breath and smiled. He was Happy again, and in that moment, he saw something behind him....

He turned around and saw his mother and the pride standing there! Happy shouted, "Mom!" His mother said, "Happy!" " We have been searching for you for a long time. When you left the pride all of the happiness left too. We would like you to come back and teach us how to be happy. "

"Sure, I will," said Happy. "And the first thing I will teach you, is to pay attention to the way you feel!"

The End

CPSIA information can be obtained
at www.ICGtesting.com
Printed in the USA
LVHW071431070519
616940LV00037B/758/P

9 781982 225865